2⁵

MAGAZINE
Behind the Scenes at **Sports Illustrated**

Books by William Jaspersohn

A Day in the Life of a Veterinarian

How the Forest Grew

The Ballpark
  One Day Behind the Scenes at a Major League Game

A Day in the Life of a Television News Reporter

A Day in the Life of a Marine Biologist

Magazine
  Behind the Scenes at Sports Illustrated

FIRST EDITION

Library of Congress Cataloging in Publication Data

Jaspersohn, William.
  Magazine: behind the scenes at "Sports Illustrated"

  Summary: Describes a day at "Sports Illustrated"
magazine, from reporting to advertising to printing and
circulation.
    1. Periodicals, Publishing of — Juvenile literature.
  2. Sports illustrated.   [1. Periodicals, Publishing of.
  2. Sports illustrated]   I. Title.
  PN4734.J37   1983   070.5′72   82-21703
  ISBN 0-316-45815-5

MUR

*Published simultaneously in Canada
by Little, Brown & Company (Canada) Limited*

PRINTED IN THE UNITED STATES OF AMERICA

For Kenny Paul,
with affection and friendship

Special thanks also to
Tom E. and Bob M.

Magazines. Their glossy covers shine at us from newsracks; their neat pages crackle when we pick them up. Magazines. Named from the Arabic word *makhzan*, meaning "storehouse," the earliest magazines date back to eighteenth-century England.

Magazines.

Today they're a six-billion-dollar industry, with magazines published on every conceivable subject: from building, photography, and politics to dressmaking, drama, and sports. The Magazine Publishers' Association in New York City says that for the average consumer 417 different magazine titles are published in the United States alone, with circulations for some as large as twenty million copies and total audiences per issue of forty million readers. In 1981, these 417 titles published a total of 290,569,385 copies, or 17.9 copies for every adult living in the United States, and despite television's draw, more magazines are being sold in America today than in any time in its history.

Yes, magazines are everywhere, yet where do they come from? Who makes them? And how much work is involved in getting out the finished product?

In the case of one magazine, *Sports Illustrated*, its birth begins here at the Time & Life Building on Avenue of the Americas in New York City.

Sports Illustrated's offices occupy two floors of Time & Life. *Publishing*, which handles much of the business of the magazine, such as bill paying, record keeping, and advertising sales, is located on the nineteenth floor, while the *editorial offices*, responsible for the actual stories and photographs that appear in the magazine, are located a quick elevator ride up, on the twentieth.

To a visitor, *Sports Illustrated*'s hallways might seem quiet, but not so its offices. Inside the managing editor's office, for example, on this unseasonably warm Monday morning in March, a meeting is in progress that will decide the very shape and content of this week's issue of the magazine.

This editorial meeting happens every Monday morning at eleven o'clock sharp, and its twenty-plus participants include all of *Sports Illustrated*'s senior editors, its copy and correspondence chiefs, its three assistant managing editors, its art, production, photography, and research directors, and the managing editor himself.

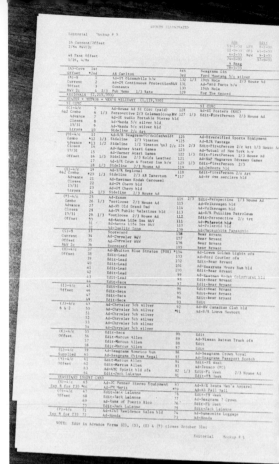

The managing editor, Gilbert Rogin, or "Rogey" as some of his staff affectionately call him, has been at *Sports Illustrated* since January 1955, when, fresh from the army and four years at Columbia College, he became a *clip boy* (a person who clips news articles for the magazine's library) at the then-starting salary of $59.50 a week. During his years at *Sports Illustrated* he's been a reporter, a writer, a senior editor, and now as managing editor, a post he's held since 1979, he not only supervises 145 editorial staffers, but also oversees and approves everything except advertising that appears in the magazine.

A few weeks ago the advertising department sent a form to the editorial staff showing where advertisements in this week's issue should run. From this *ad dummy*, the editorial staff prepared a single-page *mockup* for today's meeting, which roughly outlines where everything, ads and stories, will appear.

How are stories themselves decided upon?

As at most magazines, story ideas at *Sports Illustrated* come mainly from senior editors, though sometimes writers and photographers suggest stories, too. Since the magazine is a sports weekly, each senior editor is responsible for knowing what's happening in several different sports, and from these editors' suggestions Gil Rogin decides, week to week, which sporting events, news, and sports personalities should be covered.

The mockup can be changed if an unexpected sports story breaks, or if a scheduled story proves to be more (or less) important than expected. But today, Monday, one week from deadline, this mockup is the editors' and department heads' chief guidepost. So Gil Rogin scans his copy of the mockup and asks his editors one by one whether the stories they will oversee have been given the proper length and location in the magazine.

"Avon Tennis Finals," says Rogin. The $300,000 women's tournament is being held this week at Madison Square Garden. Gil knows that the local newspapers have been reporting that, for various reasons, several stars — Chris Evert Lloyd, Tracy Austin, Evonne Goolagong Cawley, and Billie Jean King — won't be playing. So how important is this story? How much space should it receive, and how many photographs? And should it run with the "hard news" sports stories at the front of the magazine, or the shorter "column" stories toward the back?

Ultimately, Gil Rogin alone must decide.

"How big is this tournament?" he asks.

The question is directed to Bill Colson, the editor assigned to the story. A Princeton graduate and *Sports Illustrated* reporter, who himself played stars like Jimmy Connors and Vitas Gerulaitas in Juniors Tennis, Bill is on a three-month tryout for an editorship at the magazine. Naturally, he'd like to see this story run as one of the week's leads, not because it's his story, but because he truly does feel that the tournament is important. So, to Gil Rogin's question "How big is this tournament?" Bill Colson answers, "Big. As big as the Master's in golf."

And quickly, from his corner seat in the room, assistant managing editor Mark Mulvoy says, "Yes, but the Master's has all the big names in it."

True, responds Colson, but the Avon is the only indoor women's tournament the magazine covers. In fact, it's the last tennis tournament the magazine covers until the French Open in May. It's the highlight of the women's indoor season, and this year's tournament will showcase several new faces on the tour.

"Okay," says Gil Rogin. "Sarah's on the story?" He means Sarah Pileggi, an associate writer on the magazine.

Bill Colson nods.

"Tell her we'll want her to write at least two hundred fifty lines, maybe even three hundred fifty. And John" — Gil Rogin turns to picture editor John Dominis — "we may want to do a 'gallery' of these new faces. Who's shooting the story?"

"I've assigned John Iacono," says Dominis.

"Okay, tell him shots of all the players, action and mood."

Dominis nods.

"Okay?" says Gil Rogin. "The Avon's a two-hundred-fifty-line column, though we may let it run longer, depending on these other column stories. Okay — NCAA finals!" And it continues this way through the college basketball championships, a Sugar Ray Leonard fight, a marathon in Los Angeles — every story that will run this week is discussed. Some of the stories, such as a "profile piece" on basketball star Julius Erving, are already written and ready to run. But the others, including the tennis story, won't be written until the weekend because of the scheduling of the events themselves. In fact, this week *Sports Illustrated* will extend its usual Monday morning deadline, or *close*, as it's called, to Tuesday morning so that it can run a story on the NCAA basketball finals to be played next Monday night.

Meanwhile, Sarah Pileggi is already on her way to Madison Square Garden to begin her coverage of the Avon Tennis Finals. Though matches don't start until Wednesday, a press conference has been scheduled for eleven-thirty today, and it should be a good way to talk to some of the players in the tournament.

With Sarah is Lea Watson, a reporter at *Sports Illustrated*, who, throughout the week, will help gather information for the story. Lea joined the magazine only six months ago after ten years of selling advertising for *New York* magazine. Like Lea, many writers and editors began their careers at *Sports Illustrated* as reporters. Sarah, however, despite a strong writing background (she studied at Stanford with novelist Wallace Stegner), actually started as a secretary. "I had a colossal lack of confidence," she says. But with the encouragement of several editors, she overcame her fears. After several years in the *Sports Illustrated* research department, she became a full-time writer in 1971. And now? "I feel I'm doing what I was meant to do," she says.

The press reception is already jammed with media people when Sarah and Lea arrive.

A television reporter interviews Martina Navratilova because she's played so well all winter and is ranked number one above the seven other players in this week's tournament. Another reporter chats with Rosemary Casals. Doubles as well as singles matches are scheduled this week, and Rosemary will be teamed with Wendy Turnbull of Australia.

Sarah interviews Andrea Jaeger, the youngest player in the tournament — in fact, one of the youngest professionals ever on the women's tour. Readers of Sarah's story will want to know what each player is like, so Sarah's job now is to get Andrea to talk openly about herself.

"What's it like being younger than everyone you play?" Sarah asks.

"Hard," says Andrea.

"Why?"

"Well, for one thing," says Andrea, "I can't go up to a Chrissie Evert and say, 'How'd you like to go to a movie?' because she wouldn't do it. And I can't blame her, because, if I were her, I wouldn't want to hang around with a fifteen-year-old either. Also, I feel responsible to my mother. She travels with me on the tour. I can't just walk off on her."

Sarah and Andrea talk for half an hour, Sarah writing down everything Andrea says in a stenographer's notebook. Sarah rarely uses a tape recorder on stories, feeling she listens better if she takes notes, and she doesn't use shorthand at all. "I had shorthand lessons once," she says, "but as soon as the lessons stopped I forgot everything I learned." So she takes notes in longhand, writing as quickly and clearly as she can.

Then, after a free buffet lunch provided by the tournament sponsor, the pairings for Wednesday's matches are drawn from the Avon trophy. The opening day's rounds look like this:

Round 1: Hana Mandlikova of Prague, Czechoslovakia, plays Leslie Allen of New York City

Round 2: Andrea Jaeger of Lincolnshire, Illinois, plays Bettina Bunge of Coral Gables, Florida

Round 3: Martina Navratilova of Charlottesville, Virginia, plays Pam Shriver of Lutherville, Maryland

Round 4: Sylvia Hanika of Munich, West Germany, plays Barbara Potter of Woodbury, Connecticut

Sarah and Lea note the starting time of the first match: 9:30 A.M. Then they stop by a table outside the reception room and pick up their press kits and credentials. The press kits, provided by tournament organizers, are folders containing information about the players, and they're indispensable for anyone writing about the tournament. Credentials, which consist of a green metal badge for writers and a badge with a ribbon for photographers, allow the wearer free entry into the tournament and must be worn during the matches at all times.

While Sarah and Lea get their press kits and credentials, another weekly meeting is in progress back at Time & Life, this one chaired by Philip Howlett, the publisher of *Sports Illustrated*, in his sunny corner office on the nineteenth floor.

The meeting brings together managers and directors from the publishing side of the magazine — from circulation, advertising, promotion, and business — so they can report to each other on the status of their work.

People often forget that magazine publishing is a business, concerned with making money just like any business. As publisher of *Sports Illustrated*, Philip Howlett is like a company president, responsible for the magazine's profits and losses, as well as, in his words, "creating the highest quality product at the most economical cost.

"Ours is a highly perishable product," he says. "If we deliver it late, we've got problems in that we'll be running into ourselves." So besides circulation and advertising, which are the magazine's two chief sources of income, Mr. Howlett is very concerned with the actual manufacturing and distribution of the "product."

Material for that product is being gathered throughout the week. Through officials of the Avon Finals, Sarah Pileggi has arranged for an interview with Barbara Potter, one of the new faces on the women's tour. The interview takes place Tuesday morning over breakfast in the restaurant of the Essex House on Central Park South, where most of the players are lodged.

"Tell me what it's like playing tennis professionally," Sarah says.

"Well, it *is* a profession," says Barbara, "and it takes a lot of practice. During a tournament, for example, I'll practice two hours a day, or if I'm playing singles *and* doubles, one and a half hours between matches. Then it's four hours a day the rest of the time. Now, today, I'll practice with my coach, Bill Drake, at nine-thirty, then, because tomorrow I'm playing a lefty, Sylvia Hanika, we've scheduled a practice with Martina Navratilova, who's also a lefty, at one. Then I'll eat a meal. Then, if I'm not exhausted, I'll hit again at six-thirty.

I may eat dinner in my room or at a restaurant close by, but I like to be in bed by nine-thirty or ten. I need between nine and ten hours of sleep a night when I'm on tour, eight hours when I'm off the tour. Now, going into a match, if you don't feel anything, or if you feel a little numb, the warning bells should go off; you should feel *up*. I know the particular chemistry of what's right going into a match. And then you play.

"Oh, there've been low points. But what keeps me going is the question: how would I know how good I could've been if I stop?

"I'm nineteen, sort of middle-aged as tennis goes. For me the greatest challenge in tennis is mental: the ability to concentrate and think under adversity, to merge one's self with the present and forget everything else."

"And after tennis?" asks Sarah.

"Well, I've been accepted by Princeton, and I'll probably go, but not yet."

Sarah not only writes what Barbara says, but also notes details about her, such as her skin tone, which is smooth and clear, and the color of her eyes, greenish gray. "You never know what details you might use in your story," Sarah says, "so it's important to jot down as much as you can."

Getting the interesting quotes and offbeat details for a story is part of every *Sports Illustrated* writer's job, and it often requires a great deal of traveling and interviewing. For a long piece on the Boston Red Sox, for example, staff writer Steve Wulf and reporter Bob Sullivan traveled off and on for two weeks with the team, interviewing everyone from manager Ralph Houk to former catcher Carlton Fisk to the ground-crewmen who operate the left-field scoreboard at Fenway Park. "In any piece I write," says Steve Wulf, "I'm after perspective. So I just hang around with as many different people as I can, listen, and take notes. One thing you learn: you can't go to a ballpark an hour before a game and expect to pick up a lot of interesting stuff. It's a far more complicated process."

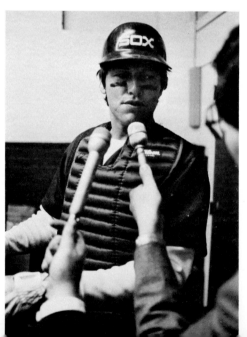

Tuesday and Wednesday are the editorial staff's "weekend" — they work from Thursday through Monday. But they're also the days that the previous week's issue of *Sports Illustrated* is printed in four big printing plants around the country.

Helping keep tabs on the printing is Merv Hyman, assistant to the managing editor and also the person who monitors all the budgets for the editorial department. Merv has been at *Sports Illustrated* since its beginning in 1954, first as a football and basketball writer, and later as chief of research before moving to his present job in 1978.

Printing goes smoothly, and by late Tuesday night all 2,325,000 copies of the magazine are off the presses and ready to be distributed nationwide.

Sarah Pileggi, meanwhile, is suffering a common writer's complaint, a case of pretournament jitters. She sleeps poorly Tuesday night, thinking about the tournament, worrying that once it's over, she won't have anything to write. "I always feel better once the matches start," she says.

Finally, they do. At 9:30 Wednesday morning, Hana Mandlikova wins the coin toss and serves to Leslie Allen of New York. Sarah and Lea take their places courtside, and the real coverage of the matches begins.

One of the benefits of writing for a major magazine like *Sports Illustrated* is that your seat at a sporting event is usually excellent. Lea and Sarah can see the court perfectly.

Sarah only notes the big points, the spectacular moments of play in the early rounds; closer note-taking comes later. For now, it's enough just to watch the matches and absorb the rhythm of play.

Hana Mandlikova vs. Leslie Allen

Andrea Jaeger vs. Bettina Bunge

Martina Navratilova vs. Pam Shriver

Sylvia Hanika vs. Barbara Potter

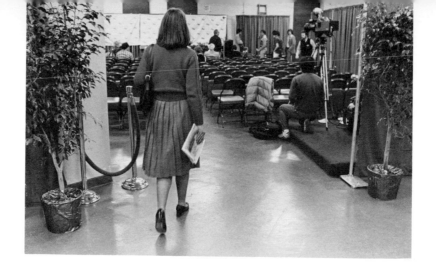

After each match, players talk with members of the media in a curtained-off section of the huge space underneath the grandstands. Sarah religiously attends every one of these press conferences because, as she says, "You never know when a player will say something important, and if she does, you don't want to miss it."

Once the writers have seated themselves, a person known as a *press representative* escorts the player to a raised table complete with microphones called a *dais*, and the press conference begins.

Hana Mandlikova has lost the first round to Leslie Allen, and one glance at her face tells you she isn't happy with the outcome. Sarah knows Hana from having written an earlier story for *Sports Illustrated* about Czechoslovakian tennis players. She has the highest respect for Hana's abilities. "She's such a marvelous athlete," says Sarah. "She's a wonderful tennis player to watch, whether she wins or loses."

The gathering for this press conference is small; it's easy to ask questions of the players. Come the weekend, though, and the semifinals and the finals, the press area will be packed with writers, all vying for the players' attention. Generally, Sarah finds New York "a tough place to do a story, because there's so much competition from other writers and so many more time demands put on athletes."

Another player who loses the first round is Barbara Potter; Sylvia Hanika beats her 6–2, 6–0. "Nobody said that this was going to be a Garden of Eden," Barbara says at her press conference. "If I can play tomorrow's round the way I know I can, though, watch out." Writers who saw Barbara nearly beat Tracy Austin at Wimbledon six months earlier nod in agreement.

After their press conferences, players shower and change in a locker room nearby, then get something to eat at a buffet table in the players' lounge, which also has pinball machines, color televisions, and electronic video games.

So that writers don't have to leave the Garden during matches, the tournament sponsor provides food and beverages for everyone wearing a press badge. Sarah stops by for a much-needed cup of hot coffee.

Nonreporting celebrities show up for the opening round, too. David Hartman, who hosts TV's "Good Morning, America" show, drops by for a chat with some of the reporters, while Sarah and Steve Flink, an editor from *World Tennis Magazine*, talk with Ted Tinling, the public relations liaison for the tournament. Ted is also a fashion designer who's designed tennis apparel for every woman tennis star since 1952. He's probably best remembered for designing a tennis dress complete with lace panties in 1949 for a player named Gussie Moran, but he's also designed wedding gowns for Chris Evert Lloyd and Bjorn Borg's wife, Mariana Simionescu.

While Sarah returns to watch more matches, Lea Watson interviews another of the tournament's newer players, Bettina Bunge, whom the press kit reports was born in Switzerland, grew up in Peru, where her father was an importer, and now lives in Florida. The interview goes awkwardly, and Lea can't understand why. Her questions are good, designed to let Bettina talk, but Bettina, polite though she is, hardly answers them. Is she shy? Lea wonders. Or does she lack experience talking to reporters? It's hard to tell. She did just lose her opening-round match to Andrea Jaeger. Perhaps her mind is on that loss?

Sarah says that some athletes have special policies for meeting the press, and at certain times they just won't give good interviews. For example, Ivan Lendl, the Czech tennis star, prefers not being interviewed at all during a tournament. "Once a tournament's over he's quite pleasant to talk to," Sarah says. Perhaps Bettina, then, approaches interviews the way Ivan does.

One player easy for Lea, Sarah, and everyone else to interview is Leslie Allen of New York City. A few weeks earlier, Leslie won the Avon Championships of Detroit, and this morning she has beaten Hana Mandlikova in the opening round. "Can you tell us how you got started in tennis?" Sarah asks.

"Well, I retired from tennis when I was eleven," begins Leslie. "Then I tried it again when I was thirteen, but retired again. It just didn't interest me — wearing those little dresses and hitting a ball. I swam all summer in Florida when I was fourteen, and when I was fifteen I did backpacking in Vermont. My senior year I was looking for an activity. I couldn't twirl a baton; I wasn't good enough to sing in the choir. Tennis was suddenly a hot sport. So I went up to my closet, and there was my tennis racket — same racket, same strings as when I was eleven. I started playing. I made the girl's team in my school, and I thought if I was good enough to get a ranking, I could get a scholarship. Then in college, I thought, if I could get good enough, I could go on the circuit."

She shrugs as if to say, "So here I am."

"And after tennis?" Sarah asks.

"I'm interested in communications," says Leslie. "If someone thinks I'm good enough, that's something I might do."

By midafternoon the opening-round matches are over, and Andrea, Leslie, Martina, and Sylvia have all won. The tournament's format is *double elimination*, meaning a player must lose two matches before she is out of the competition, so today's losers still have a chance to win it all.

Sarah and Lea now leave for the day. Sarah returns to her apartment to continue work on another story she's writing for a future issue of *Sports Illustrated* — this one about a sailboat in California that Humphrey Bogart once owned.

Lea, meanwhile, goes back to her office at the magazine and from her notes types a report for Sarah on Bettina Bunge. The information in the report will help Sarah write her story about the tournament.

Thursday morning. Free time for Sarah: round two of the tennis tournament doesn't begin until six this evening. But for others at the magazine, Thursday is a busy day. In the letters department on the nineteenth floor, staffers are answering the hundreds of letters that pour in weekly from readers all across the country. Mostly the letters contain comments about recent issues of the magazine, but others are requests for sports information, for copies of old stories, even for tips on how to become a writer for *Sports Illustrated*.

The person who first sees the letters — and answers all requests — is Bob Canobbio. He sorts the letters by subject, noting which recent stories have stimulated the most mail, then hands the sorted letters to the department manager, Ann Scott.

Ann then picks the most interesting letters and hands them in the form of a report along with the others to *Sports Illustrated*'s letters editor, Gay Flood, who's been at her job since 1960. Ultimately it's Gay's task to choose the letters to be printed in each week's issue, and she tries to select the liveliest, most representative, accurate, and informative ones for the two pages allotted her in the magazine.

Gay sees the most mail, both favorable and unfavorable, after the magazine publishes its women's swimsuit issue in early February. Generally fall and winter are her two busiest seasons because that's when more sports are being played. "Readers don't let us get away with anything," she says. "If we make mistakes, we hear about them, which is good — it keeps us on our toes."

Another department busy this Thursday morning is circulation, whose director is Bob McCoach. Most magazines rely upon subscription sales for part of their income, and *Sports Illustrated* is no exception. Its weekly circulation is 2,325,000 copies, of which 2,225,000 go to subscribers. To bring new subscribers to the magazine (and keep old ones), Bob and his staff prepare mailouts, set up telephone subscription campaigns, arrange television spots, and place ads in weeklies such as *TV Guide*. Today Bob checks the final version of an ad that will run in *TV Guide* in two weeks.

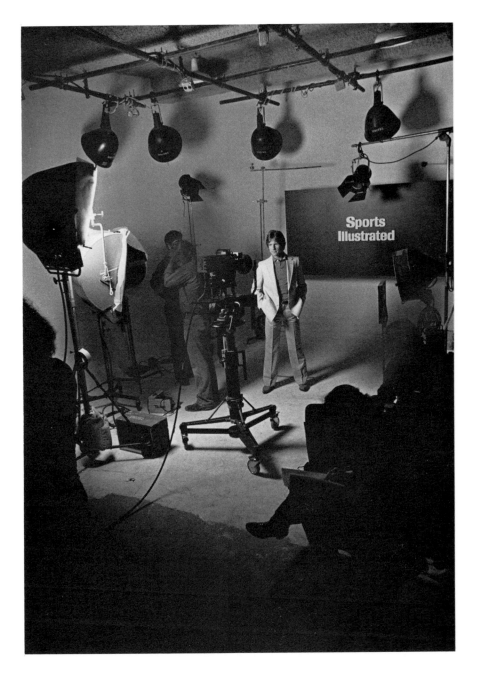

A few weeks earlier, Bob and his staff wrote a television commercial that was taped in a private New York studio. An advertising agency hired by *Sports Illustrated* helped organize, or *produce*, the commercial, and an independent film company hired an actor and did the videotaping. Though expensive to produce (this one cost nearly $30,000), such commercials are a quick means of bringing tens of thousands of new subscribers to the magazine.

Magazines also make money by selling space in their pages for companies to advertise their products. *Sports Illustrated* has advertising salespeople in eight major American cities whose job it is to convince potential customers to buy ad space in the magazine, rather than somewhere else. They do this by using charts prepared by *Sports Illustrated*'s marketing department that show who the magazine's readers are, where they live, what their average income is, and what their tastes and interests are. From attending such *flip-chart presentations*, advertisers decide if and when they want to place their ads.

To an outsider, magazine advertising might seem expensive: a full-page, four-color ad running once in *Sports Illustrated*, for example, costs $55,730. But men like Jim Hayes, who is *Sports Illustrated*'s advertising manager, and Don Barr, its associate publisher and advertising director, point out that that amounts to a few dollars per one thousand people reached, or less than a penny per person. Don Barr's words apply to every major national magazine when he says, "When you buy a page of advertising with us, you're really buying audience."

Helping to advance the magazine's name among advertisers is the promotion department, headed by Harry J. Rubicam. Harry and his staff provide the advertising sales team with materials it might need to make a sale, including flip charts, slide displays, even multimedia productions using film, music, and voice.

Busy as ever in his shirt-sleeves, today he helps the department's creative services manager, James Ferris, prepare a slide show for an advertising sales meeting in Detroit.

Bob Miller is the business manager at *Sports Illustrated*, the person concerned with all the financial matters of running the magazine. Printing costs — paper and postage especially — are soaring; the editorial department needs two million dollars annually just to cover the expenses of putting writers and photographers in the field. It's Bob's job to draw up reasonable departmental budgets so that expenses can be met, editorial can have the money it needs to put out the best possible magazine, and the magazine can still show a profit.

One of the most exciting departments to visit at *Sports Illustrated* is *enterprises*, where all the posters, games, and books that sell under the magazine's imprint originate. The man who coordinates the creation of these products is Tom Ettinger, who this morning is checking samples of a new batch of posters that the magazine will sell by mail. As Tom explains, enterprises tries to develop products that, in his words, "are logical extensions of the magazine's authority or expertise." In the future, those products will include limited edition artwork on all major sports subjects.

Keith Morris often appears on radio and television. As *Sports Illustrated*'s special-events director, Keith interviews hundreds of sports celebrities annually, and the tapes of these interviews air nationwide on the radio five days a week. Keith also oversees *Sports Illustrated*'s speaker's bureau, which arranges speaking engagements for hundreds of professional athletes.

In his office he checks to make sure his tape recorder is working properly before taking a cab to a midtown restaurant to interview football star Tony Dorsett.

Every major magazine has a publicity director, and *Sports Illustrated*'s is Jane Gilchrist. As the title suggests, Jane's job is to generate favorable publicity for the magazine, and its editorial staff and business people. She does this in many different ways. On Mondays, for example, she wires newspaper offices and television and radio stations across the country about upcoming *Sports Illustrated* stories that might be of interest in their particular region, and she's always arranging for members of the *Sports Illustrated* staff to be interviewed.

One of Jane's biggest assignments is coordinating details for the Sportsman or Sportswoman of the Year Award ceremonies. Every December, the managing editor of *Sports Illustrated*, with suggestions from the readership and editorial staff, chooses the year's outstanding sports figure for "symbolizing in character and performance the ideals of sportsmanship." The winner receives a copy of a Greek amphora, as well as the prestige of winning the award.

Surely the most popular award winner in recent years was the United States Hockey Team, which won the gold medal at the 1980 Winter Olympics against the favored Russian team.

After receiving the award from *Sports Illustrated*'s publisher, Philip Howlett, in a ceremony on the eighth floor of Time & Life, team members met with the press. "How does it feel to be Sportsman of the Year?" a reporter asked Jim Craig, the U.S. Team's goalie.

"It doesn't mean as much to me," said Jim, "as it does to all the people who got me here. My family, my coaches, my recruiter, the team's coach, Herb Brooks — it's a chance for all these people to be proud."

"Have you guys changed much?" someone else asked team captain Mike Eruzione.

"In a way," said Mike. "We're no longer the young naive college hockey players that we were before. Now we're a market and people want a part of it. I guess personally I don't want anybody to take advantage of what I think are nice people."

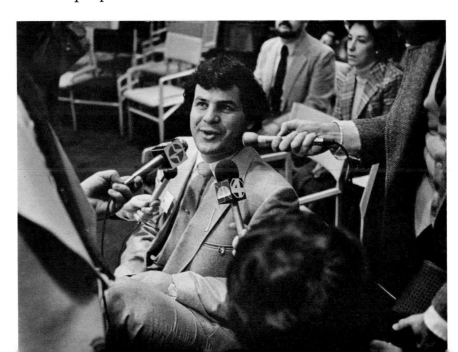

Ed Swift was at the award ceremony. A *Sports Illustrated* writer who himself played hockey for Princeton, Ed wrote the cover story about the U.S. Team that appeared in the magazine's December Sportsman issue. He traveled three weeks to interview half the team for the story, flying from New York to Switzerland to Finland to Los Angeles to Pittsburgh to Boston, then back to New York. Kathy Blumenstock, a reporter for the magazine, interviewed the other team members, and from the sixty-odd pages of notes collected, Ed wrote the story in three days. "One reason the hockey team did so well at the Olympics," says Ed, "is that they're such well-adjusted kids. This was an All-Star team, but Herb Brooks didn't treat it as such. They've certainly taken all the publicity from winning in their stride."

The day after the ceremony, Jane Gilchrist arranged for team captain Mike Eruzione and the U.S. Team assistant coach Craig Patrick to appear on a number of different television shows in New York. "The experience since winning the gold medal has been nice," said Mike between appearances. "People have been nice. The only thing I wish is that people might ask me different questions. I get tired of answering the same ones all the time."

Sarah Pileggi does television appearances occasionally. In fact, on this Thursday afternoon, she and Neil Amdur, who's a sports writer for the *New York Times*, are guest panelists on Larry Merchant's show, "Sports Probe."

Larry's guest, Billie Jean King, is someone Sarah's written about for years. Neil and Sarah ask her various questions about the state of women's tennis.

After the show, Billie Jean and Sarah just chat. One worthwhile part of being a writer for a magazine like *Sports Illustrated* is that you get to know professional athletes as human
beings. "In general, I find them amazingly organized people,"
says Sarah. "Being a professional athlete means gearing your
life to a set of priorities that are most effective toward attain-
ing your goal, and then sticking to them. Even the youngest
athletes I've met are very grown-up and efficient."

On Thursday night, with Sarah and Lea Watson watching, Hana Mandlikova defeats Pam Shriver 6–2, 7–6; Bettina Bunge eliminates Barbara Potter from singles 6–3, 6–2; Martina Navratilova beats Leslie Allen 6–3, 6–0; and Andrea Jaeger tops Sylvia Hanika 6–2, 6–3.

More photographers show up to cover tonight's action than yesterday's. They represent newspapers and magazines from around the country, and some have even come from as far as Germany to shoot the matches.

An official in charge of the courtside photographers' benches makes sure that every photographer gets a seat and that no one uses flash, strobe, or lights at any time. Tournament rules also state that motor-drives, which automatically advance film in a camera and tend to be noisy, cannot be used during serves (or at any other time if a player objects), and that no photographers can shoot from the side of the court where the players rest between sets.

John Iacono shoots the tournament for *Sports Illustrated*. A staff photographer with the magazine for two years, John brings three of his own Nikon F-3 camera bodies with him when he goes on stories, plus an array of Nikkor lenses. For close-ups of the players, he uses a big, telescope-like, 500-millimeter lens, which he steadies on a collapsible aluminum stick called a *monopod*. For wider views his other two Nikons are mounted with 105- and 200-millimeter lenses, respectively.

Light is always a big concern for magazine photographers. *Sports Illustrated* prides itself on the quality of the color photographs it runs, so to get the best possible pictures in Madison Square Garden's rather dim light, John shoots with a fairly light-sensitive, or *fast*, color slide film called Ektachrome 400. John checked out eighty rolls of it this morning from Time & Life's film lab on the twenty-eighth floor. Whatever rolls John doesn't use must be returned.

Friday morning. A busy one for the editorial staff. At eleven, Ken Rudeen, an assistant managing editor who's been at *Sports Illustrated* since 1954, chairs a meeting to plan what should run in the magazine over the next six weeks. Of course, certain stories are automatically scheduled: the "hard news" stories about events planned well in advance, such as the Super Bowl or World Series. But other stories in *Sports Illustrated* are the result of writers' and editors' batting around ideas, many of which are presented at the six-week meeting.

Thursdays and Fridays are also good days for Gil Rogin to approve pictures and layouts for any finished stories that are scheduled for future issues. Today, with Julia Lamb, a senior editor, and Harvey Grut, one of the art directors, Gil approves the layouts and pictures for a story about a mountain-climbing expedition in New Guinea.

Other editors have different routines, depending on the stories they're responsible for. Larry Keith, *Sports Illustrated*'s college basketball editor, phones senior writer Curry Kirkpatrick in Philadelphia, where Curry will cover the NCAA basketball semifinals Saturday night and the finals on Monday. Since Curry will have only a few hours after Monday night's game to write his story, he and Larry carefully discuss how long the story should be and what aspects of the semifinals and finals should be highlighted.

Meanwhile Bob Brown, *Sports Illustrated*'s motor-sports editor, edits a feature story about a stock-car driver on one of the magazine's video-display terminals. The story, by a *Sports Illustrated* writer, was written "from the field" on a portable electronic keyboard similar to Bob's, then transmitted by phone line to a computer wired to Bob's machine, where it was stored until Bob was ready to edit it.

Such equipment, gradually being introduced at the magazine, has many time-saving features, among them the capability to tell an editor that a story is too long or too short for the space allotted to it.

Preplanning at the magazine occurs whenever possible. Jule Campbell, *Sports Illustrated*'s fashion editor, and Sharon Mouliert, her assistant, are already starting work on next year's swimsuit issue. Each November, models wearing the latest-style swimsuits are photographed in tropical locations, and the pictures appear in the magazine in February. But even now, eight months before the next shoot, Jule and Sharon must begin deciding which new swimsuit styles the models will wear.

"I try to choose swimsuits that are honest, fresh, and original," says Jule, who keeps her own sketches of suits that designers show her in a thick, oversized workbook. In October she'll fly to the chosen location to select shooting sites. "You have to preselect sites," she says. "Each model's paid two thousand dollars a day, so choosing the sites early and keeping a tight schedule are crucial."

Jule's not the only one who preplans photography. For the NCAA basketball semifinals to be held tonight at the Spectrum in Philadelphia, a member of *Sports Illustrated*'s photography staff named Lou Capozzola is busy this Friday morning installing powerful electronic flash units called *strobes* on each of the arena's four light platforms. The strobes, which are synchronized to fire simultaneously when a photographer presses the shutter-release button of his camera, can be activated either by radio signal or by wire, and their light helps guarantee the crisp, beautifully colored images for which the magazine is famous.

Remote-control photography plays a vital role in many of the stories *Sports Illustrated* covers. For sporting events like the Kentucky Derby, where photographers can't be everywhere, remote-control cameras are mounted, days in advance, along the track rail and then fired by a single person using remote-control switches for dramatic pictures of key moments during the race.

Besides sporting events, *Sports Illustrated*'s photographers are often assigned to photograph sports personalities. A few weeks ago, Lou Capozzola helped staff photographer Walter Iooss, Jr., on assignment at the Spectrum, to photograph Philadelphia 76ers' star Julius Erving. The same strobes to be used during Saturday's NCAA game were brought down on court, and a white bedsheet stretched between metal stands served to screen the strobes' harsh light.

Before shooting, Walter and Dr. J. discussed the shot Walter wanted: a floor-level, wide-angle-lens view of the Doctor doing one of his famous slam dunks.

When everything was ready, Walter stretched out on his back at the edge of the key, Dr. Jr. took a position at mid-court, and the shooting began. Over and over, Dr. J. ran, jumped, floated, and at the last second made the slam dunk. "He's the true gentleman," says Walter of the Doctor. "And nobody plays the game of basketball like he does. He has that special ability to soar through the air and handle the ball like it's a peanut. He's incredible!"

After the slam dunk sequence, Walter took a portrait shot of Dr. J.

One of Walter's pictures of the Doctor doing his slam dunk is scheduled to run this week in the back of the magazine, in a profile story about the Doctor called a *bonus piece*.

Walter, who, at thirty-eight, has been a photographer for *Sports Illustrated* for twenty years, says it's always exciting to see his work published in the magazine. His advice to a young person interested in a sports photography career is, "Be patient. Work at perfecting your skills. When you're old enough, get involved taking sports pictures for a newspaper or wire service. Build a strong portfolio of your work, with a combination of action and quieter shots. A lot of photographers can shoot only one or the other. In my opinion, the person who can shoot both has everything he needs to get a job at a place like *SI*."

For the NCAA semifinals on Saturday night, *Sports Illustrated* has two photographers shooting the action.

The matchups for the semis include Virginia versus North Carolina and Indiana versus Louisiana State; the winners of those games meet Monday night to decide which team will be national champion.

Curry Kirkpatrick is the writer covering the semis. A senior writer at *Sports Illustrated* who began as a reporter in 1962, Curry has a tricky assignment. He must write one story that will cover both the semis and the finals. So, to make his job a little easier, he will write the middle section of his story concerning the semis right after those two games. Then, after Monday night's final, he will write the rest of his story.

Sarah Pileggi has decided to handle her tennis story much the same way. On Friday, Martina Navratilova, Bettina Bunge, Sylvia Hanika, and Andrea Jaeger all advanced to the tournament semifinals. Today, Saturday, Navratilova and Jaeger win their matches and become the tournament finalists. They will face each other on Sunday afternoon for the $100,000 first prize.

After Saturday's semifinals, Sarah goes back to the Time & Life Building to write everything she can about the tournament, including today's action.

She writes until 2:00 A.M. Then she goes home to her apartment, gets four hours' sleep, and returns to her office to write some more. By eleven o'clock Sunday morning, she has drafted the middle part of her story.

Meanwhile, at around ten on Sunday morning, Andrea Jaeger practices for her finals against Martina Navratilova by rallying on the main court with her good friend Pam Shriver. Before matches players can also work out in another part of the Garden known as the Felt Forum. Don Candy, Pam's coach, watches this warmup from the sidelines.

Then at one-thirty, with the crowd of 14,000 seated and ready, Martina and Andrea walk to center court, where dozens of photographers take their pictures.

The coin toss is next; Martina wins it, and elects to serve. A few minutes later, the finals begin.

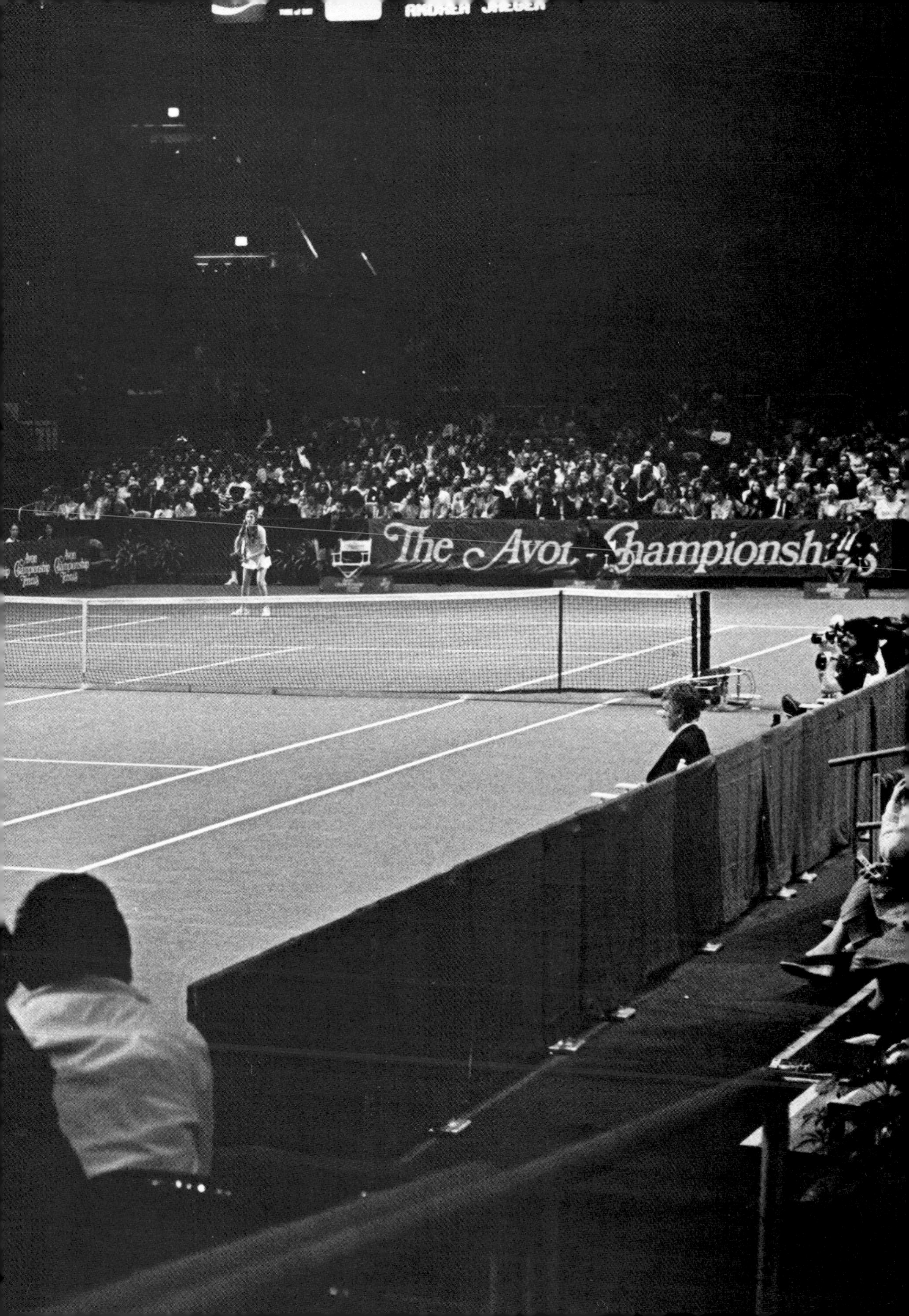
ANDREA JAEGER
Avon Championship Tennis

Andrea is known as a patient player who hits from the
baseline and waits for her opponent to make mistakes. To
break this pattern, Martina's strategy is to draw Andrea to
the net with short dropshots, then hit the ball past her as she
tries to rush back into position.

The strategy seems to work. Martina wins the first set
easily, 6–3.

Sarah and Lea take close notes on the finals. Sarah records every point played, using her own improvised scorecard, and jots down her impressions of the players and the match.

John Iacono is back to take pictures. All told, by the end of the tournament, John will have shot some sixty rolls of film, or almost two thousand pictures.

The match itself takes less time than expected. Andrea fights valiantly against Martina's grueling attack, but it's clear, today anyway, who the stronger player is. Martina takes the second set with a tie breaker, 7–6, and by winning the match, wins the tournament! The crowd applauds and cheers.

After the award ceremonies on court, where Andrea receives a check for $52,000 and Martina receives one for $100,000, the two players are escorted back to the press area, which, this time, is bristling with reporters.

"Andrea, do you think one of your problems today was coming to the net?" a sportswriter shouts.

"Yeah, coming to the net," says Andrea, nodding. "I think once I start playing doubles it'll help my net game."

"Martina, you looked more relaxed and confident out there than I've ever seen you before," says another reporter. "Has your attitude about playing changed?"

"Once you're on the court it's always enjoyable," says Martina, "but now I like it [playing] better than ever."

69

When Martina and Andrea move on to interviews for radio and television, many of the print reporters start writing their stories in a place called a *pressroom*, set up by organizers of the tournament. Typewriters for reporters who didn't bring one are located there, as are telephone hookups to anywhere in the country. And when reporters finish writing, they use machines called *telecopiers* to relay their stories to their publications.

Sarah decides to finish her story back at the office. But first she chats briefly about the tournament with John Iacono, who's on his way to deliver the film he shot to the Time & Life film labs.

Next, in a quiet corner of the press area, Sarah listens to a tape recording of the press conference. Tournament officials make the tape available to all reporters, and Sarah listens to it to make sure she didn't miss any important quotes.

The subway ride and walk back to her office take Sarah just twenty minutes. A moment later, at her typewriter, she starts writing again — slowly at first, just a few words at a time. But before long the pages start filling, and Sarah tapes them to her office wall along with what she wrote last night to see how the story's shaping up.

"I don't outline," she says. "I find outlines too constricting. But I do have a theme in mind when I sit down to write. In this case it's that Martina's dominated winter play, and that the tournament this week was a showcase for lesser-known players. Besides those themes there are always a certain number of facts that have to be included in any story, such as who won and what the score was."

Sarah says that getting everything into the space she's allotted — in this case 250 lines — is never easy. But she also says that the exhilaration she feels when she finishes a good story makes all her hard work worthwhile.

Other staffers on the magazine are rushing to finish their stories, too. Herm Weiskopf, who writes "The Week," a column summarizing the week's major baseball, basketball, or football games, gets most of his material from a nationwide network of correspondents for the magazine, known in the trade as *stringers*. The stringers, who usually work full-time for local newspapers, phone in their reports by Sunday morning, and it's Herm's job to compress this information into a column as much as 500 lines long. He also selects the Player of the Week based on stringer suggestions, box scores, and newspaper stories.

Jerry Kirshenbaum writes and edits the "Scorecard" section of the magazine. A former *Time* staffer who came to *Sports Illustrated* in 1969, Jerry, too, relies on stringers for much of his material, though he also reads ten newspapers daily and stays abreast of wire copy for interesting sports items. " 'Scorecard' is sort of a catchall department for things that don't fit in the rest of the magazine," says Jerry. "In it we include both light and serious items, and we also use it as our editorial page to comment on sports-related issues."

"For the Record," a summary of the week's events in all major sports, is also put together from stringer reports, wire service information, and phoned-in scores. Reporters are assigned to edit the column for stretches of three to six months, and the current "Record" editor is N. Brooks Clark. He's also responsible for one of the most popular sections of the magazine, a photo gallery of the week's outstanding amateur athletes called "Faces in the Crowd." Each week, some fifty "Faces" suggestions from readers arrive at *Sports Illustrated*, and from these Brooks chooses the six that will appear. Each athlete chosen receives a small silver bowl from the magazine, and though the column's purpose isn't to spot tomorrow's stars, several former "Faces" including Arthur Ashe, Tracy Austin, and Nancy Lopez, have gone on to become cover subjects of the magazine, and seven — Chris Evert Lloyd, Jerry Lucas, Rafer Johnson, Steve Cauthen, Neil Broten, Jack Nicklaus, and Terry Bradshaw — have gone on to become Sportsman or Sportswoman of the Year.

Not all writers this weekend are working in their offices. Several, like Curry Kirkpatrick at the NCAA finals in Philadelphia, Kenny Moore at the Los Angeles Marathon, and Pat Putnam at the Sugar Ray Leonard–Larry Bonds fight in Syracuse, New York, are doing their stories from the field. A few, like senior writer Frank Deford, who's just finished a long piece on Chris Evert Lloyd, do much of their writing at home. The Evert Lloyd story is a future bonus piece. "I've done about sixty of them by now," says Frank, who started at the magazine right out of college in 1962. "The story took almost three weeks. I saw Chrissie three times: once for a formal interview, next in Tampa, where she and I watched her husband play tennis, and last in Boston, where she was the one playing. I do a lot of research on a subject *before* I meet her, and for the actual writing I like to leave two weeks. But it never actually takes me that long, usually three days each for a first and second draft."

Home is also where the Connecticut artist Walt Spitzmiller works. Though not affiliated directly with the magazine, Walt is often hired as a *free-lancer* to create artwork for the magazine's numerous feature pieces. Today he is working on a series of paintings for a picture spread about rodeos.

The well-known author, television personality, and founding editor of *Paris Review*, George Plimpton also writes sports pieces as one of eight special contributors, or *contract writers*, for *Sports Illustrated*. "I'm paid a certain amount each month," says George. "The ideas for stories are usually my own, but if I don't come up with my own, the editors at the magazine come up with ones for me. I'm not good at writing to deadlines; I'm more of a distance writer. A bonus piece of four or five thousand words takes me three to four weeks." Nevertheless, George Plimpton usually has five or six writing projects going simultaneously, most of which expand to become books. When asked how he manages to get all his projects done he replies, "I get verbally whipped by editors asking 'Where's the story?' So I give a terrible cry and find myself working all night."

At six-thirty Sunday night, when Sarah Pileggi finishes her story about the tennis tournament, the manuscript goes to Bill Colson, *Sports Illustrated*'s tennis editor, who makes minor corrections and changes in black pencil, then sends the manuscript to the terminal room. There, one of five typists, who can type about ninety words a minute, feeds the story into a terminal connected to a computer six floors above.

The computer, housed in a room called *copy processing*, stores the story and *typesets* it, that is, puts it into the form and typeface in which it will eventually appear in print. A *copy processor* makes six copies of the typeset story, and a computer clerk whisks the copies down to *Sports Illustrated* via a pneumatic mailing tube.

The first, or *top*, copy of the story goes to the *copy editing* department, whose chief of fifteen years is a personable woman named Betty DeMeester. Betty or one of her eight staff members reads and *edits*, or corrects, each story that comes in for mistakes in spelling, punctuation, and grammar. Little escapes their close attention, and whatever they don't understand in a story gets a question, or *query*, penciled beside it.

Copy editing takes special talent; for one thing, you must know how to spell. Betty gives every new copy editor she hires a spelling test, and the list includes both misspelled and correctly spelled words. Do you know which is which? Betty asks.

> *accommodate   priviliged   paralel   obbligate*
> *flambuoyant   desicate   supersede   harass   embarrass*
> *judgement   rarefied   liquefy   tranquility*

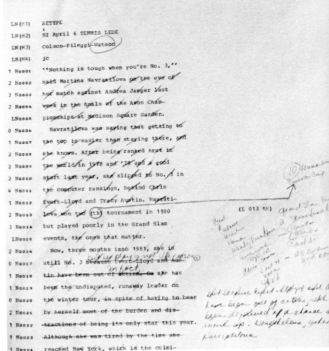

One of a reporter's main jobs at the magazine is checking stories' facts, and since reporter Lea Watson worked all week with Sarah Pileggi, tonight she checks the facts in Sarah's story about the tennis tournament. She does this mainly by consulting record books and phoning players and tournament officials, but if it's appropriate, she can always go down the hall and use the *Sports Illustrated* library.

By the time Lea is finished, she will have checked every word of Sarah's story.

And what about the photographs that John Iacono took at the tournament? After leaving Sarah, John dropped the film off at the Time & Life film lab where it was developed, checked for flaws, cut and mounted in slide holders, then packed and delivered via dumbwaiter to *Sports Illustrated*'s offices.

The lab, which handles both color and black-and-white film, is one of the most modern of its kind, and it's also where film for *People*, *Time*, *Discovery*, *Fortune*, *Life*, and *Money* magazines is processed. Each magazine pays the costs for its own pictures; the average weekly run of Ektachrome film for *Sports Illustrated* alone is five hundred rolls. In addition, each week the magazine shoots another five hundred rolls of a film called Kodachrome, which the lab ships to the manufacturer for processing. In all, *Sports Illustrated*'s photographers shoot over thirty thousand pictures a week (ten thousand were taken at the Super Bowl alone), of which perhaps fifty are actually published.

John Iacono's slides of the tennis tournament go to the magazine's picture editor in charge of tennis, Barbara Henckel. She does a *rough edit* of the pictures, choosing from John's two thousand shots the hundred or so better ones that illustrate the tournament. Of these, *Sports Illustrated*'s picture department head, John Dominis, chooses the two dozen best, which he arranges in a slide tray for showing to Gil Rogin.

The slide show, known as a *color meeting*, takes place in a conference room directly across from Gil's office. Members of the art, editorial, research, and production departments are also present to critique the slides, but, as with everything else that appears in the magazine, the final decision on which pictures run rests with Gil. How many pictures will finally accompany Sarah's story? Only two: one of Martina Navratilova and one of Andrea Jaeger in their finals match.

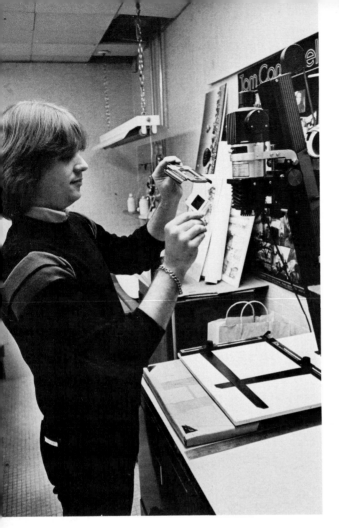

Those two slides go to the *production department*, where
Pieter Muuse puts them in a machine called a *photo enlarger*
to make what is known as a *paper negative*. When the room
is darkened, light from the enlarger is allowed to pass through
the slide and is focused onto a piece of light-sensitive paper
mounted below. The paper, with the image of the slide on it,
is then processed in a *developing machine*, and, a few minutes
later, Pieter has paper negatives of each slide.

With these negatives and with information he received from the copy department about the story's length, Rick Warner, *Sports Illustrated*'s assistant art director, begins sketching the design, or *layout*, of Sarah's story as it will actually appear in the magazine. "I must think of three things when I sketch," says Rick: "the amount of space I have, the way the pictures look in relation to each other, and the overall pacing and design I want to achieve."

Once he's done these sketches, known as *thumbnails*, Rick transfers the design to a *layout page*, which exactly duplicates the size of two pages in *Sports Illustrated*. By knowing where he wants the photographs to run on the page, and by using a movable sizing device, Rick can gauge exactly how big the photos for the story should be. He takes this information a few doors down the hall to Pieter Muuse in production.

Using the negatives and another machine in his arsenal called a *sizing machine*, Pieter makes *paper positives* exactly to Rick Warner's specifications. They're ready in a matter of minutes.

Next, art department staffer Cathy Smolich, using the sized positives and Rick's sketches, does the first *paste-up* of the actual layout. She doesn't paste in the words in Sarah's story yet — this layout is just for seeing how the page will look overall. Instead, Cathy uses scrap pieces of column from past stories and random headline letters (called *dummy type*) in the style Rick specified, and pastes these where Rick's sketches show they should go.

When she finishes pasting up the layout, Cathy takes it back to Rick, who shows it to Dick Gangel, *Sports Illustrated*'s art director. Dick may make suggestions for improving the layout — changing the pictures' sizes, moving the dummy type elsewhere, making more room for the *captions* that Gil Rogin and assistant managing editor Peter Carry will write for each picture. In such cases the layout goes back to Cathy or Rick. But once Dick Gangel gives his approval, the layout is taken to Gil Rogin, who passes final judgment. When Sarah's story is finished being edited, Rick and Cathy will put the layout in its final form, pasting the actual words and headlines of the story into place. Later, this final layout will aid printers and other production people in seeing how the pages are supposed to look.

Eight o'clock. Because the Time & Life cafeteria is closed at this hour, and so that staff members won't have to waste time leaving the building to eat, an old Sunday night tradition at *Sports Illustrated* is a buffet supper, served by a private caterer in the conference room where color meetings are held. Tonight's menu: lasagne, Italian bread, salad, milk or coffee, brownies, and fresh fruit.

On lasagne night, most everybody, including Gil Rogin, has seconds.

After supper, Lea Watson discusses her fact checks with Gil and Peter Carry. The fact-checking has gone smoothly; Lea's done her job. Her fact corrections now go to the copy department, where Betty DeMeester or one of her staff will insert them in the top copy of Sarah's story.

Then Sarah's story, with its factual corrections and with changes that tennis editor Bill Colson has made in black pencil, moves on to others in the editorial department. Jeremiah Tax, a former assistant managing editor and now special contributor to *Sports Illustrated*, does his editing (in this case revising and rewording) of Sarah's story in blue pencil, and an hour later Gil Rogin does his in red. Why so many editors for one story? Why so much checking and correcting? Because, says Gil Rogin, compared to a newspaper, "the standards for a magazine are higher; it should be better than a newspaper. It should have better pictures, better writing, *and* better editing. People reading the magazine expect it, and we feel they deserve to get it."

The result of all these high standards is a finely polished story, but the editorial process doesn't stop here.

```
LN(#1)    RETYPE
LN(#2)    SI April 6 TENNIS LEDE
LN(#3)    (Colson) Pileggi-Watson
LN(#4)    jc

1 N0001   ``Nothing is tough when you're No. 3,''
2 N0002   said Martina Navratilova on the eve of
3 N0003   her match against Andrea Jaeger last
2 N0004   week in the finals of the Avon Cham-
LN0005    pionships at Madison Square Garden.
0 N0006     Navratilova was saying that getting to
1 N0007   the top is easier than staying there, and
2 N0008   she knows. After being ranked first in     — getting off to
2 N0009   the world in 1978 and '79 and/a good
2 N0010   start last year, she slipped to No. 3 in
4 N0011   the computer rankings, behind Chris
1 N0012   Evert-Lloyd and Tracy Austin. Navrati-
2 N0013   lova won two         tournament in 1980    (L 013 t)
3 N0014   but              in the Grand Slam
LN0015    events, the ones that matter.
2 N0016     Now, three months into 1981, she is
0 N0017   still No. 3                but her play is not the reason. In fact,
1 N0018   tin have been out of action. So she has    But because Evert-Lloyd
1 N0019   been the undisputed, runaway leader on      and Austin have been at
0 N0020   the winter tour, in spite of having to bear  action, she has been deprived of
2 N0021   by herself most of the burden/and dis-      a chance to move up. Nevertheless,
1 N0022   tractions of being its only star this year.  when Navratilova
1 N0023   Although she was tired by the time she  arrived in
1 N0024   reached New York,            the culmi-
```

STXT0010 262,851   PAGE   2

```
0 N0025   nation of Avon's 10-week winter circuit,
1 N0026   she was as relaxed and confident as she
2 N0027   had been in a long time. She stayed at
1 N0028   the quiet and very tory hotel Carlyle on
1 N0029   upper Madison Avenue instead of at the
1 N0030   Essex House in midtown where the oth-
1 N0031   er players lodged, and she and her com-  NOVELIST
0 N0032   panion,              Rita Mae Brown,
4 N0033   found time to see a Broadway show
2 N0034            a mov                        STET
1 N0035
```

Before the night is over, Sarah's story will be retyped and rechecked at least three more times. Eventually, one of seven pairs of *proofreaders* will read it, one to the other, to make sure that all changes have been incorporated correctly. The same procedure will be used for every other item in the magazine — from "Scorecard" to the fight story, which was written last night, to "Faces in the Crowd" — every last word will be checked.

All through Sunday night into the wee hours of Monday morning as the editorial process goes on, pictures for this week's issue are prepared for printing at a company in nearby New Jersey called G. S. Lithographers.

G. S.'s job is to translate the week's photographs into a system of tiny colored dots that a printing press can print on paper. Upon receiving a batch of the week's slide pictures by car from *Sports Illustrated*, technicians at G. S. put each slide on a complex and expensive machine called an HCM-HELL 300-B *laser scanner*. As every art student knows, in printing you can make any color of the rainbow using different combinations of three colors: red, yellow, blue, along with black. The scanner separates the tones in a slide into these colors, and breaks each color into a system of dots. The slide's colors, in dot form, are exposed separately on photographic plates called *film*; the four plates are developed, and several copies of each plate are made in an adjoining room. When the developed plates are sandwiched one atop the other, a beautiful enlargement of the original picture — in dots, and to the size *Sports Illustrated*'s art department specified — appears.

Later, when it comes time to print this week's issue of *Sports Illustrated*, these dot-covered pieces of film will play an important function.

Nontransparent illustrations, such as paintings and drawings, go through the same four-color, dot-separation process on this huge camera-like machine.

 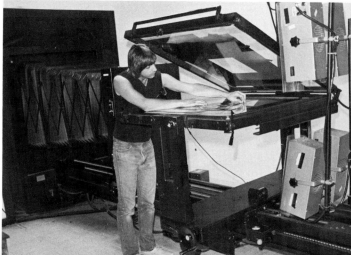

Any film that needs retouching (to soften or enhance its colors) goes to the *etching department* at G. S. There, specialists delicately retouch the dots, using fine brushes dipped in a chemical solution.

The stripping department then *strips*, or puts together, all the pieces of film to make sure the dots for each picture match up properly and the colors look as they should.

Once plates are ready for the week's issue, they are shipped to the four regional printing plants in one of two ways. Pictures to the plants in Los Angeles and Chicago are sent from a sophisticated computer scanner in New York, which beams the picture signals to the plants via an earth-orbiting communications satellite. Pictures to the plants in Atlanta, Georgia, and Old Saybrook, Connecticut, though, are bundled in big tan envelopes and flown directly from New Jersey by chartered plane.

Monday night. And because of the NCAA basketball finals, the magazine is still "open" and the editorial week is now eight days old. But in a few hours the national championship game between the Indiana University Hoosiers and the University of North Carolina Tar Heels will be over, and Curry Kirkpatrick, *Sports Illustrated*'s senior writer covering the event, will be able to finish his story.

As tip-off time approaches, the air at the Spectrum in Philadelphia is electric. Horns hoot, bands blare, fans cheer. Huge, goofy red foam "Hoosier hands" inscribed "Go Big Red!" wave throughout the arena, and North Carolina girls, their faces painted with cute little powder-blue feet, with a black "tar" spot on each heel, jump and scream. *Everybody* who cares about college basketball is present. The noise is deafening!

Blocking out the distractions as he prepares his scorecard and notebook for the game is Curry Kirkpatrick. He has already written and shipped to New York the middle part of his story (about the NCAA semifinal games held here Saturday night). Tonight he will have just one hour after the game to write the 150 lines that make up his story's beginning and end. Before the game Curry admits that for him, "It's kind of a nervous time. The NCAA finals are different from any story I do all year. I'm aware that I'll have only an hour to write. Fortunately, since it's an event, a game, the story kind of writes itself. I don't need any special strategy."

Someone who's been helping Curry gather quotes this weekend and who'll be gathering more from players and coaches after the game is Bruce Newman, a staff writer who also covers college basketball. Both teams tonight are guaranteed fair coverage in the magazine because Bruce is an Indiana graduate while Curry graduated from North Carolina. Nonetheless, "Doing interviews gets tougher all the time," says Bruce, "because we're now competing with so many different media for the athletes' and coaches' attention. Interviewing's not the free lunch it used to be; now you've got to beat the other reporter."

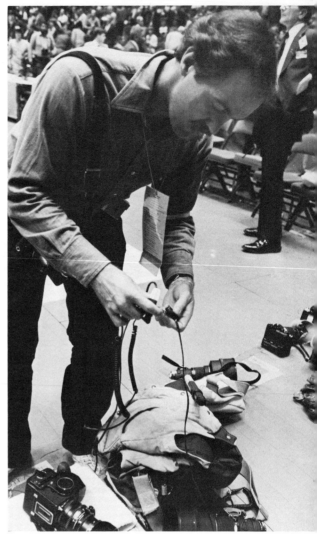

Hoping to shoot the best pictures of the game are Rich Clarkson, a contributing photographer for the magazine, and staff photographer Manny Millan. Besides action pictures, both Rich and Manny will be looking for postgame victory shots, one of which will serve as this week's cover photo of the magazine.

Manny plugs a wire from his camera into an outlet running to the strobes installed on the Spectrum's light platforms last Friday afternoon. Every time Manny presses the shutter-release button of his camera, all four strobes will fire simultaneously, flooding the arena with a sharp, even light, essential for fine color pictures.

The game moves sluggishly at first. Each team either misses or trades baskets in what seems destined to remain a low-scoring game. At the end of the first half, Indiana takes the lead, their first of the game, 27–26. And then in the second half, the total Indiana game — the balanced shooting and smothering man-to-man defense — comes alive. Led by brilliant guard Isiah Thomas's game-high 23 points and by the excellent defensive play of guard James Thomas, Indiana wins the national championship, 63–50.

The Hoosiers, fans and players alike, go wild.

After the game, reporters swarm through the dressing rooms, interviewing anybody and everybody they can. Many, writing to newspaper deadlines, interview for only a short while before heading off to write their accounts of the game in a dressing room that's been converted into a press area for the championship.

Curry interviews out on the floor for only five minutes before dashing upstairs from the court to a small pressbox on the mezzanine, which, to his surprise and relief, is unoccupied. Moments later, his notes, scoresheet, and pages of writing spread alongside him, Curry writes the rest of his story.

"Writing doesn't come easy for me," he says. "I'm probably the world's slowest bleeder. It always takes me a long time to get into a story, yet once I do, it starts to go. And throughout it all, I'm always calm. It always comes."

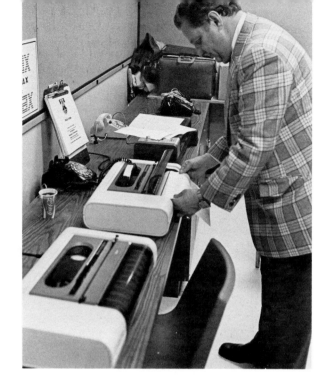

An hour later, when Curry finishes his story, he takes it into the adjoining *wire room* where a man from Amfax Communications sends it to *Sports Illustrated* by means of a telecopier. The telecopier converts Curry's letters and symbols into electronic signals, and a telephone receiver, inserted into the machine, carries the signals by wire to New York. There, a similar machine in *Sports Illustrated*'s offices converts the signals back into letters and symbols, and each page, just as Curry typed it, is printed.

The technology for shipping film back to New York is less refined and far more complicated. When Manny and Rich finish photographing the victory celebration, each puts his film from the night into specially marked envelopes and hands them to an assistant from the magazine. The assistant steps outside the Spectrum, where a motorcyclist, hired for the night, is waiting to whisk him through traffic to the Philadelphia airport. A chartered Learjet is waiting there; the assistant will fly to New York, take a cab to the Time & Life Building from Kennedy Airport, and have the game film in the lab by 1:00 A.M. By 3:00 A.M. Gil Rogin and his editors will be choosing pictures for Curry's story.

The person who actually receives Curry's story off the telecopier is Eleanore Milosovic, *Sports Illustrated*'s chief of special correspondents. Besides receiving stories from writers in the field, Eleanore and her staff of five coordinate communications with the magazine's network of stringers, often even calling correspondents based abroad for any information the magazine requires. As soon as Curry's story is received, Eleanore makes photocopies of it and distributes them to Curry's editors on the floor.

Meanwhile, from his room in the Franklin Plaza Hotel in Philadelphia, *Sports Illustrated* reporter Roger Jackson has already begun the difficult job of checking every fact in Curry's story just as Lea Watson did for Sarah Pileggi's tennis piece. Roger talks mainly with NCAA officials, verifying the statistics and manner of scoring for each team. But for background facts he's armed with record books and with phone numbers of the schools' sports information directors, and, in all, he'll be on the phone tonight for over five hours.

All through the night, the editorial process spins on. Larry Keith (the senior basketball editor), Gil Rogin, and Peter Carry mark up, comment upon, and agonize over every word in Curry's story. Peter and Gil divide up the captioning chores, each editing the other's captions for the story's pictures. Gil chooses this week's cover shot: a photo by Manny Millan of Indiana guard Isiah Thomas triumphantly scissoring down a basket net after the game. The slide is whisked away with the others Gil selected for color separation at G. S. Litho, and a short while later Gil approves the art department's layout for the cover. Everybody's exhausted but nobody admits it. Finally, at 6:00 A.M., Curry's story, all 352 lines, reaches the last, or *final copy*, stage of editing. So, twenty hours after they came to work (and on only four hours' sleep from the night before), Gil Rogin and his editorial team can "close" this long-open issue of the magazine. It's time to shut down the twentieth floor of *Sports Illustrated* for its oddly scheduled midweek "weekend." It's time this week's issue of the magazine is printed and shipped!

Crucial tools in *Sports Illustrated*'s creation are computers. Once a story has been approved by editorial, it is typed for the last time into the twenty-fourth floor's big copy-processing computer, which is capable of many complex tasks. Among its features is the capability to instantly *set* a story, including black-and-white photographs, in the form and typeface in which it will be printed, leaving only the color work for G. S. Litho to do. It can produce beautiful, full-size, transparent black-and-white film reproductions of any page, called *proofs*. And, with just the push of a button, it can electronically store and transmit a story to other computers in exactly the form in which it will appear.

Once a story is set in its final form, it travels electronically from Time & Life's copy-processing department to another computer outlet on Pine Street, sixty blocks south. There, Time, Inc. staffers check the computer-made transparent proofs of the story against the final layout to make sure that both agree. The layouts, which are actually photocopies of the art department's originals, are delivered to Pine Street by cab.

After layouts and transparencies are checked, the story passes through a system of computers located nearby and, like the printing plants, owned by the R. R. Donnelley Corporation. When the time comes to move a story to the Donnelley plants, a computer technician phones each plant one by one and asks if it's ready to receive a transmission. When a plant official answers "Yes," the technician *patches*, or connects, a cord from the computer into a telephone panel connected to the plant. A few button pushes later, the story — in this case, Curry Kirkpatrick's — is on its way over the phone lines to the printing plant hundreds of miles away. The last phase in the birth of this week's issue is about to occur.

The 700,000 copies of the magazine distributed in the Northeast are printed at the Donnelley plant in Old Saybrook, Connecticut. A computer there receives the Pine Street transmission, and a technician, using the computer's capabilities, makes transparent film "proofs" of the story — both negatives and positives — exactly like the ones used at Pine Street for checking.

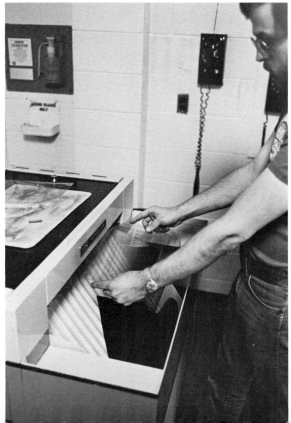

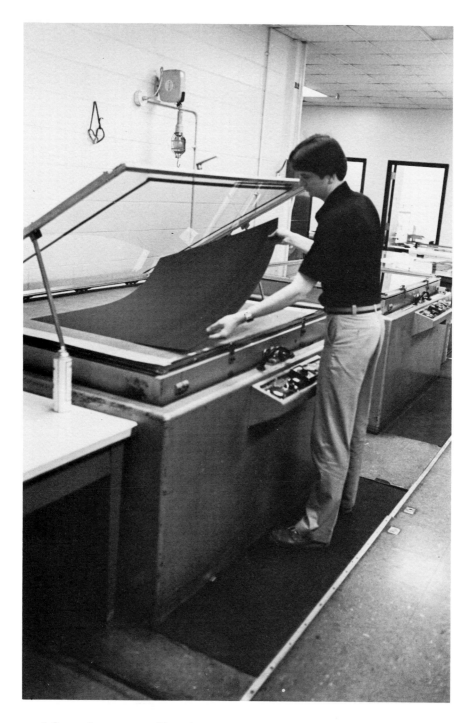

After the story film has been matched up with the color film from G. S. Litho, the negatives of each are laid separately on the light-sensitive surfaces of special aluminum plates. The plates, with the film on them, are exposed to ultraviolet light inside huge tables, called *vacuum frames*, and after about two minutes' exposure, the plates are developed and washed.

This process cleans away the material in the nonexposed areas of the plates. When the developed surface is dried and allowed to harden, the exposed areas become *ink-receptive* and *water-repellent*, while the nonexposed areas remain the opposite. In other words, ink will stick *only to the exposed areas of the plate*. This becomes important when the plate is put on the printing press, where both ink and water are applied to it.

When the plates are developed and their surfaces hardened, they are bent along one edge on *plate-bending machines*.

And then, each in turn, the plates are locked onto the smooth steel rollers of one of several printing presses in a giant area of the plant called the *pressroom*.

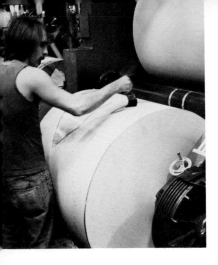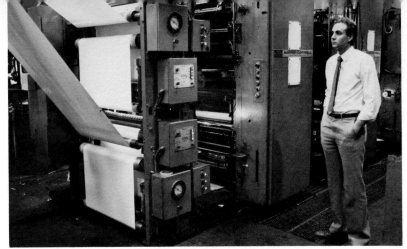

Paper for the presses comes in huge rolls, each weighing over a ton, and the rolls are attached to arms on the presses called *spiders*. Each roll holds enough paper for a twenty-minute run, but the presses are designed so that they can keep running even while new rolls are spliced onto the old.

Pages in *Sports Illustrated* with color pictures on them are made by passing paper through each of four units on the press. Each unit holds two printing plates, and each plate is usually inked with only one color. As the paper moves through each unit, a new color is printed over the previous one: first blue, then red, then yellow, then black. These four inks combine to create any hue a picture needs, and thanks to those film separations that G. S. Litho made, each color appears on the paper as a system of tiny dots.

This four-color press is called an *offset press* because its plates never touch the paper but instead transfer ink to rollers over which the paper passes. The Donnelley Company has presses whose plates *do* touch the paper; they're called *letterpress presses*, and they're used for black-and-white and two-color pages.

The inked paper zips through a line of gas furnaces fired to a temperature of 600 degrees Fahrenheit. The heat dries the ink, and a series of water-filled *chill drums*, over which the paper passes next, sets the ink so it won't smudge when handled.

Then the paper is automatically cut down the middle to form what pressmen call *ribbons*, and the ribbons are halved again, into strips called *dinkies*. A machine near the end of the press called a folder cuts and folds these dinkies into eight-, sixteen-, or twenty-four page groupings called *signatures*, and a worker loads the signatures on *pallets* to ready them for their last stop, the bindery.

In all, the offset press can make 18,000 to 24,000 impressions every hour, and the total time it takes to print those 700,000 weekly copies of *Sports Illustrated* is approximately 42 hours.

The bindery machines, on which the signatures are assembled into finished magazines, operate a bit like automated clotheslines. Employees called *feeders* start with the signatures that go in the middle of the magazine and work outwards, feeding the signatures into twenty stations along the line called *pockets*. The machines pluck a single signature from the first pocket, drop it on a thin, conveyer-like chain, and zip it down to the next pocket, where the second signature is placed piggyback-style atop the first. The machines repeat this signature-stacking function all the way down the line, with the cover, which was printed on heavier paper, going on last.

Afterward, a *blow-in card machine* feeds subscription cards into designated pages, a stapling machine staples all the signatures together, and a set of three guillotine-like blades trims the pages, leaving the finished product we know.

A single binding machine can produce 8,000 to 10,000 magazines an hour, and with three machines working at once, the job goes fast and smooth.

Wednesday night. In all four plants, the finished magazines are pouring off each line at the rate of 150 a minute. Labeling machines in each plant are automatically pasting on the address labels of *Sports Illustrated*'s 2,225,000 subscribers, and workers are bundling and bagging those subscriber magazines according to ZIP codes and carrier routes. "We do half the post office's work," says an employee at one plant; the other half is done after the postal trucks come and cart off the magazines for mailing.

Earlier, privately owned tractor trailers came and took away those 100,000 magazines destined for stores and newsstands. By midnight Wednesday night all that's left after the last magazines go out the door are the page trimmings. These the printing plants crush into refrigerator-sized bales, which paper companies buy and make into toilet paper, ceiling tile, and tissue paper.

By Thursday morning, those 100,000 retail copies of *Sports Illustrated* have been shipped from the printers' by truck to over 200 *news distributors* nationwide. The distributors' job is to deliver the week's issue wherever magazines are sold, and most distributors have lists of regular customers.

So at last, on Thursday afternoon, the magazine — with Curry Kirkpatrick's basketball story and Sarah Pileggi's tennis piece and Walter Iooss, Jr.'s picture of Julius Erving — at last, that magazine with those and other stories and pictures has finally gone out into the world. Writing, photographing, editing, printing, and distributing this week's issue have required the efforts of thousands of people — along with a matchless technology, and not a little timing and luck.

In New York, at *Sports Illustrated*'s headquarters, copies of all the week's stories and layouts have been placed in an envelope and stored with past *carbon files* in an air-conditioned vault on the twentieth floor.

Around the offices, it's almost as if last week is forgotten, because everyone — editors, writers, photographers, and business people — are off and running on a new issue. To do their work they *must* forget and set their sights ahead. Monday deadline is just five days away.

Another new issue of the magazine must be produced.

Acknowledgments

This book could not have been written without the help and co-operation of numerous people at *Sports Illustrated* and elsewhere. I especially wish to thank Merv Hyman, a wonderful, patient man, who was my liaison with the magazine's editorial department, and who, in the course of my work on the book, became not just a helpful adviser but a friend. Merv retired from his position as assistant to the managing editor just as this book was going into production. I wish him a joyous and fruitful retirement; my gratitude for his help is inestimable.

That gratitude extends to others in the editorial department, especially Sarah Pileggi, Lea Watson, and Curry Kirkpatrick. Curry's patience in letting me observe him at work was above and beyond duty, and Sarah and Lea were by far the kindest and most cooperative subjects that this writer has ever met. If this book shines at all, it is in Curry's, Sarah's, and Lea's reflected glow.

From the first day we met, Gil Rogin made me feel welcome in his domain. His openness in letting me sit in on and photograph editorial meetings was exceptional, and I will always cherish memories of watching "Masterpiece Theatre" in his office on Sunday nights while we talked about the magazine and he waited for fresh copy to arrive.

Ken Rudeen, too, let me sit in on several Friday editorial meetings, and along with Peter Carry and Mark Mulvoy, was always supportive while I was working on the book.

The *Sports Illustrated* art department became something of a home away from home for me, and Dick Gangel, Harvey Grut, and especially Rick Warner deserve my hearty thanks. Rick generously designed the layout that appears on the title page of this book, and also arranged for me to meet one of the magazine's most talented contributing artists, Walt Spitzmiller, with whom I had a happy interview at his home in Connecticut. Cathy Smolich and Pamela Fortson, also in the art department, answered many technical questions for me, and, in production, Gene Ulrich, George Infante, and Pieter Muuse showed me how the magazine's pages are actually prepared for the printer.

I could not begin to mention everyone I worked with in editorial, but I do want to give special thanks to Lester Annenberg, Bob Brown, Jule Campbell, Lou Capozzola, Brooks Clark, Rich Clarkson, Richard Colan, Bill Colson, Robert Creamer, Frank Deford, Betty DeMeester, John Dominis, Gay Flood, Clive Gammon, Barbara Henckel, John Iacono, Walter Iooss, Jr., Roger Jackson, Diane Johnson, Larry Keith, Jerry Kirshenbaum, Julia Lamb, Scot Leavitt, Doug Looney, Betty Marcus, Linda-Ann Marsch, Joe Marshall, Manny Millan, Gloria Muuse, Craig Neff, Bruce Newman, George Plimpton, Bob Sullivan, Ed Swift, Jeremiah Tax, Ken Tomten, Herm Weiskopf, and Steve Wulf for letting me interview and photograph them.

On the nineteenth floor, in the publishing department, my great good thanks go to Philip Howlett for so graciously taking the time out of his busy schedule to meet with me. The rest of the publishing staff, particularly Bob Miller and Tom Ettinger, were always kind and cooperative, and Jane Gilchrist warrants special thanks for arranging so many appointments for me. Thanks, too, to Don Barr, Jim Hayes, Bob McCoach, Harry Rubicam, James Ferris, Keith Morris, Bill Ely, and Ann Scott and their staffs for their special cooperation and help.

I also wish to thank the following people outside the magazine's offices for *their* special contributions to this book:

In copy processing: Michael Keene, George Austen, and the entire copy processing staff

At G. S. Lithographers: Joanne Nebus and the entire G. S. staff

For expert cab driving: Barron Cooper

At the Pine Street offices: Jim Wagner, Charles Patton, Dennis Nosal, and the copy transmission staff of R. R. Donnelley

At the R. R. Donnelley plant in Old Saybrook, Connecticut: Bob Pitts and the entire Donnelley staff

At Time, Inc., manufacturing, Saybrook division: George Baldassare and Jerry Kleutsch

At Fifty-seventh and Second: Al Siegel

From Great Performances Artists-as-Waitresses Catering Service: Celia Hughes

From Coane Productions, Inc.: Jim Coane, Kristina Gutkowski, and their staffs

At Fenway Park: Jim Healey, Ralph Houk, and the park ground-crew members

At Burlington News Agency: Roland Berube and Mark Merchant

At the Avon Tennis Tournament: Ted Tinling, Peter Bodo, Barbara Potter, and Steve Flink

At "Sports Probe": Larry Merchant, Maide Oliveau, and Billie Jean King

At "Good Morning, America": David Hartman and his staff

At Cable News Network: Debbie Segura

At Wunderman, Ricotta, and Kline: C. Texas East

For the Philadelphia 76ers: Julius Erving

For the Chicago White Sox: Carlton Fisk

For the United States Olympic Hockey Team: Mike Eruzione and Jim Craig

Love and thanks also to:

Ward Rice, of the Camera Store, Stowe, Vermont, for darkroom wizardry unexcelled

Gerry Paul, for recollections, suggestions, and friendship

Dr. and Mrs. Peter Cunningham, for a home away from home

My parents, Paul and Dorothy Jaspersohn, for unstinting support and love

Last, but first always, love to Pam and Andrew.

Blessings, all.

        —WJ